STUFF

TALES FROM PLACES

Red Engine Press
Fort Smith, Arkansas

Library of Congress Control Number: 2023944577
ISBN: 979-8-9879576-6-0

Cover Design by Aaron Logan Ray
Cover art by Cody Banning
Editing by Todd Fischer

CONTENTS

A SWIFT SWORD

Chaleron ran a stone over the pitted blade. He smiled down at the steel. The light of the setting sun made the metal and his hair flare the color of flame.

"Why not marry it, Chal?" the pinkish-furred creature sitting across the campfire said. A smirk on the face of a two-foot tall squirrel is almost as disquieting as it is adorable. She poked the fire and shook her head.

"She has gotten me through a lot of scrapes. Even if she isn't as hale as she once was, she's an ally — inanimate or not," Chal answered, pushing the stone the length of the blade.

"Why do boys always gender their weapons? And why are they always female? Sexist," The squirrel called Ruffpinkle spat into the fire.

"You have a point, Ruff. Still, she is a strong lady to me and I respect her. I'll reforge her, too," Chal said.

"You could have given 'her' a better name. Gulwilde the Weaver? It doesn't even tick the alliteration box," Ruff said, shoving the stick she'd been poking at the fire with into the ground. With a gesture, she lit the electric blue orb on the end, giving them some extra light in the growing darkness.

"Okay, Ruff the Rascal, what's your staff's na—" Chal began as an arrow thudded into his shoulder from the nearby treeline. He looked at it wide-eyed for a fraction of a second before he raised Gulwilde, whose blade glowed as he scooped Ruff and her stick up. In a blink they were behind a line of mercenaries, just inside the same trees the arrow had flown from. The spot the pair had been standing a second before was now riddled with feathered shafts.

Chal dropped Ruff quietly and teleported behind the closest cutthroat, sliding Gulwilde into the brigand's side before the blade's glow could alert anyone.

The orb on Ruff's staff glowed blue, and lightning struck the thug farthest to Chal's left. The ionized bolt forked out and turned two more of the enemy party to crisps.

"I guess they've never heard our names!" Chal yelled, teleporting around, killing all but two archers and one half-giant.

The big man laughed, "We've heard your names, Chaleron the Swift. You, the rat and the sword. Now we have all three." His bearded face lit up from the dull red glow of his axe as he slammed it into the ground. A crack opened up in the earth and snaked angrily toward Chal.

"No thanks," Chal said, blinking to the man and clanging Gulwilde's blade against the large axe. The crack retreated, the axe went dark and slid back into the half-giant's hands as he shifted back to a ready stance with his head thrown back in laughter. Large, heavy-browed eyes went wide as Chal brought Gulwilde up under giant chin through to less-giant brain.

Chal pulled the blade free, slung the gore off, and

2

brought the hilt to his shoulder. The blade shone white-bright and the arrow that had been lodged in Chal's shoulder thunked harmlessly into the ground where he had been standing before the short skirmish.

Chal looked at the remaining archers, "Well? Run," he said. They obliged with no more than a whimper.

"You know it's Lundrich. He knows you want that hammer, and he is going to keep sending people after you until you confront him." Ruff said, paws on her hips. Her robes' trim was still glowing with spidery, blue runes.

"Then he'll send them. I'm not going to confront him. I'm going to steal the hammer to reforge Gulwilde." Chal said with a smug grin.

"We're not rogues or thieves. You don't know the meaning of the word stealth, and you speak like a two-shike bard." Ruff said.

"Stealth. Noun. Cautious or surreptitious action or movement. I choose to think I'm quite ear-pleasing, and your assessment of those mercenaries gives me an idea. We're going to walk into his castle and take it." Chal grinned even more smugly.

"Don't blame me for any of your hair-brained schemes! You're just going to waltz in the front door of the most heavily guarded fortress this side of the Gloaming?"

"Nope," Chal said, "We are. And, you're right. We do need a thief. I know just the one. Maybe a decent bit of muscle, too."

"You're bad at—" Chal snatched the squirrel up by the hood of her robes and teleported into the distance.

———

The fire troll Beeth lumbered through the Lundrichtowne marketplace. At nine-feet tall and five feet wide, he made a comfortable seat for the four foot tall fae lounging across his shoulders as he carefully plowed through the busy crowd in the royal city's marketplace.

"Excuse me. Sorry. Oop! I'm so sorry!" Beeth bellowed as he bent down to check on a shopper whose foot he'd trod on. "I'm very sorry. Would you care for a sweet?" He reached into a pouch at his side and rummaged around until he came out with a candied eel head. The young woman he'd stepped on squeaked in fear and ran away. Beeth tossed the head into his mouth and crunched thoughtfully as he restarted his careful walk.

"Guess her foot was okay," the elf-like creature said from behind Beeth's massive neck, "Take a right into that alley. We're going to meet them at the tavern, as cliche as that may be. Their being in town is risky. Chal has never been known for his planning. I'm just shocked his pet rat is letting him," Fre'atha said.

"Don't call her his pet, Fre. She has a name. It's Ruffpinkle. People call me your pet because they think I'm dim. It's not right," Beeth said.

"Okay, Bee. I'm sorry," she said as she ruffled the troll's hair from behind.

"Chal's gonna get caught, then Lundrich will take Gulwilde and become even more powerful," Beeth said, clearing the alley and stepping into a much less crowded town square.

The buildings on each side were made of light stone with red terra cotta rooves. A statue rose in the middle; a sneering human with a thorny crown choking the life out of a smaller man. The figure of a female orc lay on the dias beneath, a child in her arms. Both had staring, lifeless eyes that rolled back into their heads in gruesome detail.

"Turns my stomach," Beeth said, his ember-red eyes glowing as they welled up with tears.

"We'll tear it down, if all goes well. To the Tiger," Fre pointed to a sign showing a stumbling tiger, dropping a tray of ale mugs. Beeth turned out onto the wide highway that cut through the square, closing the distance to the Tripping Tiger Tavern in a handful of huge strides.

At the door, Fre slid down from Beeth's shoulder. "Why do we always meet in taverns? Why do you always hear about heroes in stories meeting at taverns or pubs," Fre said as she stepped toward the door.

"They are public places. It is less conspicuous than the back room of a dungeon or something," Beeth said. Fre shrugged her lack of disagreement. "Wait," said Beeth, raising an eyebrow and stopping Fre in her tracks, "Are we the heroes?"

"Just this once, Bee. C'mon," Fre said, opening the door to the tavern.

————

Chal and Ruff flickered solid ten paces north of Lundrichtowne's east gate. They could've blinked right up to the tavern, but Lundrich had express orders for his town guard to arrest anyone that teleported within the city walls. The kingdom was unsafe for practitioners of any temporal art thanks to Emperor Lundrich's vendetta against Chal.

Ruff waved her paw, and they became a young girl and a pink-haired house spirit just before they came into view of the gate guards. The guards asked their business. They answered that they were headed to the market and the soldiers lazily waved them through. Within three minutes — and many curses about having to move so slowly — Chal and Ruff arrived at the front door of the Tripping Tiger. They saw Beeth squeezed behind a table in a corner.

Ruff scooted into a chair next to Beeth, and Chal sat opposite her. Fre looked up from the tulip wine she'd been drinking. "Hello little girl, how can we help you?"

"Stuff it up your pixiedust chute, Fre. You know who I am. Can we please go? Steal a hammer and ruin a dynasty?" Chal asked, looking disgruntled.

"He can't do his boop-boop-poof thing in town, can he!" Beeth laughed.

Ruffpinkle tried to keep a straight face, "No, he's such a big baby. He complained the whole way here," she laughed.

"You don't want to wait for some special moment? Sleep on it?" Fre asked Chaleron.

"I slept on it last night, after the bastard had sent a detachment of cutthroats and a bintzing half-giant with a named weapon to kill me," Chal said.

"Who was it?!" Beeth asked.

"It was Gorfthak the EarthBreaker. They said his skin was made of stone, but Gulwilde slid into his head like butter," Ruff said.

"Yes. SHE's Gulwilde the Weaver, alright" said Chal to Ruff, then turning to Fre, "I have thought this through. Lundrich will be at the market, doing some kind of speech in about a quarter hour. A lot of the town guard will be there with him and the hammer will be in the castle with only his mage guarding it. This is the smoothest sailing we're gonna get," Chal said.

"I think it's a half-cocked plan, and I think you being in

town is suicide, but we're with you. Bee?" Fre asked, turning to the troll.

"That mage is a fire-mage, anyway. Weak as a little baby against me. I guess Chal has done some homework," Beeth said.

"He copied off me," said Ruffpinkle, smirking.

"Let's just go, please," Chal said, standing.

"Wait a second," Beeth said, "I ordered duck!"

"Yeah, we're waiting on our food. That's a condition," Fre said. And they waited. Chal sulked.

————

The streets were crowded with market day revelers heading to hear their king. Evil as he was, he put on a good show. Chal continued to complain until they reached the keep wall.

"Can't I just climb over?," Beeth said regarding the wall.

"The wall has anti-climbing spells and—" Ruff was cut off by Chal.

"And we're burning daylight," Chal strode over to the gates. "Excuse me mister, but this troll accidentally threw my dolly over the wall. Could you go get it?"

The guards looked at each other and both laughed, "No," said the one to Chal's left, "Go away, little girl," both guards laughed heartily.

"Suit yourself," said Chal the little girl. Chal drew Gulwilde as the form of the little girl melted away to reveal Chal not-the-little-girl. He blinked behind the guards and took both of their heads in one swipe. "Come on!" he shouted to the others.

Inside the gates they noticed there were many less guards

than they'd expected. In fact, they saw none. Only a man washing the castle windows on the second story.

"Just in case," Fre said, raising both hands then dropping them slowly. The party's forms shimmered and four town guardsmen stood in their place. One of the dead guards at the gate glittered as he became a serf. Both bodies now held bloodied blades.

As they headed up the cobblestones, they passed another pair of guards.

Chal said to the new pair of guards, "Some serf has just killed Barnaby at the gates!"

The two guards looked slightly confused, slipped on the helmets that had been under their arms, and took off toward the gates.

"Who's Barnaby?" One asked.

"New kid from over Giltstown, maybe. Probably had a purse and all, likely split it afore anyone knows!" The two guards took off at a jog.

Chal and the group entered the castle, moving unmolested, until they realized they had no idea where to go on the second story. Chal held a finger up and teleported. Half a minute later he came jogging back with the window-washer.

"Orders directly from Lundrich. Chaleron the Swift is in the area and is rumored to be heading here to steal the fabled hammer, Mord the Maker," Chal waved them on as he and the window-washer passed. He let the new man outpace him by half a step so he could follow.

After many stairs, they came to a halt at a pair of twenty-foot, steel-banded doors. Two half-giants stood in front of the gates with spears that almost scraped the ceiling. The spears crossed as the group of guardsmen — and one window-washer — came within twenty paces.

"If one of them says 'who goes there' or 'state your business', I'll zap 'em," Ruff whispered.

"Who goes there!" boomed the one on the left.

"Ugh!" said Chal and Ruff in unison.

"State your business," said the one on the right.

"Okay, look. I'm going to be frank here," Chal said, extending his hands. "We need to go into that room. One way or another."

"Frank. Do you know a Frank?" Left said to Right.

"No. Definitely not on the short list," said Right

"What was Marg's kid's name?" asked Left.

"Frakka. Not Frank at all." replied Right.

"Just drop the illusion. I can't take any more of this," Chal said. Fre waved her hands. The window-washer stayed the same because, well, he was actually a window-washer.

"Come quietly and no one—" Right and Left began to say in unison, but were stopped. One by a lightning bolt from the ceiling, the other by a jumping slash from Gulwilde.

"Will get hurt, we know," Chal said with an eyeroll.

There was a faint rattling and the party turned to see the window-washer was shaking so hard his knees were knocking together.

"Well? Run," Chal said, waving him off.

They stepped into a wide chamber. In the center, on a white dias, lay a hammer made of one piece of blue steel. A middle-aged man in red robes stood with his back to them just to the side.

"He's going to turn around and say he's been expecting us," Ruff said.

"I've been expecting—" The mage got nothing else out of his mouth, as Gulwilde lopped his head clean off its shoulders.

Chal walked over to the hammer and picked it up, laying Gulwilde on the ground near the now-headless corpse. As he hefted the tool, it began to glow, and Gulwilde's blade went dull.

The hand of the headless mage closed around the handle of the sword as it faded to plain steel. The corpse raised the blade. The head rejoined the body. The mage lept to his feet and separated both of Chal's arms just below the elbow. The mage caught the hammer as it fell, dropping Gulwilde in the process.

The red-robed man tapped the sword with the hammer and it shattered. He then tapped the sword's long-time wielder on the forehead and Chal's body went the same way as the sword.

Ruff jumped forward, the orb on her staff white-hot, but Beeth grabbed her at the last moment. The form of the red-robed mage wavered, faded and coalesced into the form of a sneering human wearing a thorny crown.

"Well? Run," Lundrich laughed. The three remaining friends wasted no time. The doors began to close behind them as they fled the treasure room, and the town guard filled the hall before them.

"Shit," Ruffpinkle said as the guards advanced toward her.

DUNGEONS & DRAGONS

I just want to play dungeons and dragons
I just want to cuddle with my girlfriend and watch
    that new Sonic movie
I really like the redesign and think Jim Carrey will kill
But, this is Capitalism, kids, and I'm an artist
So I have to drag myself to a 9-5 job so my boss can
    get richer and the kid can eat
Peas
Or some other kind of mashed up puree that
    resembles what my brain feels like after a day
    serving the corporate world
I was a newspaper reporter once
It was kind of fun until the corporate shills from
    Chicago came down and tore apart my little paper
    family because we didn't sell enough
Ads
To the endless existential fear built up by a society
    that has forgotten it used to be hairy, scared,

hiding in a cave from the cold and finding fear of
the dark

Now the fear in the dark is the stress tomorrow will
bring because there isn't enough time to love the
things you love because every second has to be
spent on the relentless pursuit of green ink on
paper that rules our lives that have been rendered
this way by green ink on paper that rules our lives
that have been rendered this way by green ink on
paper that rules our lives that have been rendered
this way by green ink on paper that rules our lives.

But at least we still have The Office, which is a show
that says all of the things we think every day in
such funny ways, then hits us with those poignant
sit-down moments where all we can do is hold our
breath to keep from crying because we've all felt
that way. And, that show spawned D&D memes,
which reminds me...

I just want to play dungeons and dragons.

THE DOG

We first noticed the dog a few weeks before summer ended.

My best friend and I had been piddling about in front of the gas station we both worked at. The dog had wandered out of the woods across the street and had flopped down just at the edge of the rural highway. We don't miss much in the half mile stretch of road that is visible before the mountain swallows the blacktop back up at either end.

The dog flopped down on the shoulder and lay there, yelping quietly and panting heavily. It was medium-sized, nondescript and black - we noticed - as we crossed the parking lot to examine it.

"Maybe someone shot it," J.W. said a little too matter-of-factly.

"Maybe, but it sure looked fine before it keeled over. I don't like it," I said.

"You love dogs. Something about this one that's specifically putting you off?"

"No, I developed a sudden and acute hate for doggo

kind. Yes! This one specifically. Before it plopped down it looked, for all the world, happy. Like..." I trailed off, trying to think what to say before some snide remark—

"Happy, tail-wagging pupper is good, right? Surely there isn't some sinister, preternature afoot." J.W. said, smirking. He always met my paranoia with Spocklike logic.

"I know what you're thinking," I said, now standing directly over the dog, "but the fucking thing was smirking. It looked pleased with itself."

As I finished my sentence, the dog quieted, opened one eye, rolled said eye, then bolted back into the woods as hale and sound as the day it was born.

"From the middle pit of Hell," I said, finishing my inner narration's sentence. "Mark my words, J.W., this is the beginning of a horror movie," I said.

"Cool. We just won't have sex or go into basements. Neither should be a problem for me, one should be easy enough for you," said J.W., pushing his thinning brown hair back on each side.

"I'd never go into a basement!" I said with mock revulsion.

"Unless there was something you could fuck in it."

"Touche," I smiled as we headed back in. "Did you see the fucking thing roll its eyes? Consider my timbers shivered." I shuddered comically.

"Probably death spasms."

"And the running away part?"

"Last bit of adrenaline," J.W. said. "It'll go die in the woods, poor thing, while you're thinking it's a hellhound. Looked to be a lab mix." J.W. opened and held the door.

"Labrador with a dash of Satan. Thanks." I said as I

stepped into the reassuring fluorescent light, "Its features were too delicate and its yelping was too human. Almost sounded like moaning. A 'keening', some'd call it" I said.

"You'd know," J.W. said, raising an eyebrow.

"I would. I know a lot about dogs. I was a v—"

"Vet tech for a while. Yup. You worked at a humane society," J.W. said.

"I could stop telling you stories," I said.

"Nuh-no," J.W said, putting a hand up, "I like your stories. Just tell some new ones. I think we have a great candidate here. A touch of embellishment and that dog could be doing a jig in the road as we speak."

I had a feeling in that moment that my best pal was gonna regret those words soon. I wish I was wrong more.

Days passed, and just short of a week later, the dog showed up during the after-work rush. A nearby, larger town has a couple factories that bacon the bread of folks that live along the red clay tributaries feeding into the highway in front of our little store.

The workers were all stopping in for the nightly fill-up and brew-down when it happened. The demon-mutt trotted into our parking lot, way out by the air machine - that is dangerously close to the highway - and plopped down. As soon as it hit the ground, I could see that one foreleg was hanging by a tendon from the elbow down. I hopped the counter and blared across the parking lot toward the dog. I didn't care if this was Beelzepup, I wasn't gonna let it suffer. I pulled out my phone as I neared a couple that had also raced over to the dog, planning to call my sister who worked in a local vet's office.

The man was scratching the thing behind its ear and

saying, "Poor puppy has a boo-boo." His female counterpart smiled sweetly and suggested they call the number on its collar (there was no collar), then she held the dog's maimed appendage in her hand as blood and gore started to spill into her hands.

"Ma'am, you might hurt it worse than—" I trailed off because I noticed the dog was smiling at me. Not the big, goofy grin a pitbull gives you, but a sly, tight-lipped smirk you get from a YA novel villain.

"Folks," I said, putting a hand on each of their backs, "I think you ought to step away from the dog. It's bleeding all over you and could have some disease you could tak—" I was cut off again, this time by the dog audibly sighing, rolling its eyes again and bolting into the woods, the leg that had been a bloody stump now propelling the pooch forward in great bounding strides.

"Oh, that's a shame," The man said.

"Bye, little guy!" The woman said, "Why would you scare him off?" She said as she slapped me on the chest, leaving a gory smear of viscera behind.

The couple meandered back to their car dreamily. I made sure they paid for gas, grabbed another shirt from the trunk of my car, and walked back into the store, wide-eyed.

"What's with them?" J.W asked as I walked in, tossing my soiled t-shirt in the bin.

"My. Sentiments. Exactly," I said. "I'm utterly unsure. I just know the dog had one leg mostly-amputated, the Stepfords there were acting like it was some sweet stray in a Disney movie, then Baphomutt smiled at me. Fucking smiled. Before you say it, no, I don't mean cute-puppy-smile like Walt Flanagan's dog or some shit. No, it smiled at me like Doctor Fucking Lecter."

"You're sure it was the same dog? I mean, what're the odds?" J.W. said.

"Someone get me a young dogcatcher and an old dogcatcher," I said, making the sign of the cross in the direction of the woods. J.W. laughed; I laughed, but the tension of the situation hung thickly in the air. There were so few ways this could end well in my mind.

"Next time it comes up, we just ignore it," J.W. said as I tossed my cigarette in the cat litter filled ashtray outside the door of the station. "Seriously, we just call the sheriff's department, say there's a stray running in and out of traffic, then we ignore it."

"Okay, man, but there's a ninety percent chance they are gonna just 'poor doggy' it like everyone else, and they'll look at us like we're somehow doing disparagement to this beast and arrest us for animal cruelty. I'm telling you, man, the thing is out to get us," I said.

"C'mon, man. It's a dog. It's not some creature feature. I know weird shit happens sometimes, but we'll just call the dogcatcher."

Another near week had passed as I stood in front of the store staring through the fog from the mountain and the curl of cigarette smoke in front of my face. I glared at that treeline like my great aunt used to glare at me when she knew I was up to no good.

"I don't think it's coming back," J.W. said from behind me, causing me to jump. "Sorry, I'll announce myself the next time you're scanning the treeline for our doom."

"Man, this has been scary. You know what black dogs dogs mean in folklore, right?" I asked.

"The grim. Hellhound. Sirius Transphobia — I mean Black. Serious Black. Yes, it has been explored. Thoroughly,"

J.W. said. "Maybe it was some kind of shared delusion,+ and the dog wasn't actually hurt. Maybe the floor cleaner fumes got to us. You did smoke a huge joint that one evening, and—"

"Okay, I get it. You're in denial. You know what you saw. The first time we could maybe write off. The second? The gory handprint on my shirt? Explain that away," I said.

"Maybe it was cut, maybe one of the people was cut. Maybe she'd been eating extra-saucy pizza. Maybe some fiend from the middle pit picked us and our backwoods gas station to terrorize." J.W. shrugged, sighed and headed to the back.

I had lit up a smoke about the time three cars pulled up. Two pulled to gas pumps, and one parked to my left, in front of the ice machine. I moved toward the ashtray to snuff the cigarette when the driver stepped out of the car, "Don't rush for me," he said as he slid a coffin nail of his own between his teeth.

"Those things'll kill ya," I chuckled.

"So I'm told," The man said, adjusting a ball cap on his white hair, then running his fingers through a well-kept - if slightly nicotine-yellowed - beard. He walked over to me and joined me in staring at the treeline, "Woods around here can be creepy as hell, can't they?"

"You don't know the half of it," I said.

"Oh, I might have an idea. Spent plenty of time in woods just like these. Strange sounds, feelings, and even stranger sights cross a man's path in there. Real Stephen King shit," he finished.

"Sounds like you might know more than the half. We've been having some dog problems and—" I trailed off as the underbrush rustled. I perked up from my perch on the sill of bricks underneath the plate glass as a lithe, black head and shoulders emerged from the woods, "Speak of the devil." I said under my breath as I headed to get J.W.

As my hand reached for the door, it flew open and J.W. dashed past me, an orange-handled machete in his hand. I started to protest, but my friend was already halfway to the road. I stood in shock for a half-second, then took off after him as my new smoking buddy let out a, "What the hell kinda—"

I broke into a run and the dog did, too. It flew past J.W. to the gas pumps and laid down equidistantly between them. As it did, it's back half disappeared, replaced by a bloody mess of ribs, spine and entrails. I skidded to a stop as J.W. ran back past me, blade held high like a dervish.

J.W. ran over, machete in hand. He was suddenly covered in blood and viscera, as was the machete, though he'd not swung it at all. He looked at me with wide eyes as a woman who'd been gassing up her overly large SUV screamed, ducked into her car, and came back up with a pink-handled .38 trained on J.W.'s head.

"Leave that dog alone or I'll shoot you, you monster!" SUV lady yelled as J.W. turned to look at her and the dog began a high, keening wail.

She stepped around the front of her vehicle and saw the back-end of the dog for the first time. The dog smiled that creepy smile as SUV Karen screamed again, "You've killed it!" She screamed, retraining the weapon on J.W.

The report of the weapon seemed deafening as I slammed into J.W. and rode him to the ground, the bullet grazing my lower back before lodging harmlessly into the concrete. The machete clattered to the ground and skidded away, clean bladed.

I could already hear sirens in the distance as I began to stand. J.W. was smooshed beneath me with a look of shock on his face, but nary a speck of gore on him. The dog, completely whole, rolled it's eyes, jumped up and ran back into the trees.

I reached a hand down to J.W. "Okay. I'm convinced, now," he said.

SUV Karen stared on, wide-eyed. Her gun still pointed in our direction. She was still standing that way thirty seconds later when a sheriff's deputy slammed her to the ground and cuffed her. She kept muttering, "I'm sorry, I thought—" as they loaded her into a cruiser.

J.W. and I didn't press charges, and the lady came by to apologize, but our boss trespassed her from the premises. We accepted the apology and the offering of lemon bars.

The Karen and J.W. had a brief discussion about the incident, and she was the first onlooker to notice that the dog ran away, whole. She asked to see my wound, and I showed her the tiny burn mark on my lower back.

"The old folks talk about demons in those woods. Things that did all kinds of unspeakable things. Y'all'd best be careful," she said, finally as the boss told her her time was up, and ushered her out the door.

J.W. was decidedly less skeptical of my 'crazy talk' and a lot more skittish. He'd now join me scanning the treeline, from time to time.

"I hope the bastard does show back up," he said one night, staring into the trees.

"Why would you say that?!" I half-screamed as I choked on my own smoke.

"Because, I'm gonna shoot it right in it's balls," he said, lifting his shirt to show the grip of a revolver sticking out of his pants.

"Woah, man. Since when do you carry?" I asked. Guns were commonplace in our state and we'd been raised around them, but J.W. had never been the type.

"Since I almost got my best friend shot. I won't hesitate putting that thing down, next time," J.W. said grimly.

Almost a full month passed with no sign of the dog, but then, one night just before dusk, J.W. flew back into the store from changing the garbage cans.

"That motherfucker is back," he yelled, skidding around the corner of the counter and snatching up his pistol from a cubby behind it. As he lit out the doors, I saw a familiar black shape part the underbrush.

A thoroughly confused customer gaped after J.W. and said, "Dog bite him or something?"

"Or something," I said, hopping the counter. "Please excuse us, that thing is dangerous. I'll be right back."

I jogged after J.W. who was already at the edge of the highway, drawing a bead as he went. The dog seemed to be waiting for him, smiling that Eldritch smile.

"Dude!" I yelled as I ran after J.W., "Careful with that thing! It already almost got you—" I was cut off by the sickening thud and screeching of tires as a car slammed into J.W. at full highway speed. The gun went off once just before the impact.

J.W.'s body flew over the windshield, shattering it. He landed in a battered, bloody heap behind it. The dog grabbed him by a mangled leg and dragged him into the bushes. J.W.'s head lolled back, his eyes locking with mine. The gun had plunked harmlessly into the underbrush.

I shook off my shock and bolted for the highway. I checked both ways then crashed into the underbrush after the dog and my best friend. I vaguely heard the man who'd hit J.W. mutter something as I passed.

I ran for the better part of two minutes, screaming J.W.'s name, but there was no sign of him or the dog, and the trail of gore stopped just inside the treeline.

By the time I got back to the road, sirens were approaching once again. The man who'd hit J.W. happened to be an off-duty cop from a town over, and his corroboration of my story helped in both getting him off the hook for the accident and sparking a three-week long search for my lost pal. They found the gun a foot from the road and confirmed one round was spent.

After the search ended, J.W.'s case was considered cold, and we never found a sign of him besides the gun.

Some weeks later while pulling into work, I found some buzzards eating the dark corpse of a black, lab-looking dog.

"Not again," I muttered under my breath, as the dog hadn't appeared again since taking J.W.

I parked and walked out to the corpse. It was very dead, torn open and half eaten by carrion birds. I slid its eyelids open and touched its eye. No movement. That meant true brain-death. Couple that with no pulse and I dragged it to the side of the road. I called the sheriff's department and let them know about the corpse, and it lay there until the street crew came by and scooped it up later that day.

"Looks like someone shot the poor ol' thing," The man in a stained orange vest said as he paid for his coffee. "People can be awfully cruel to animals."

As soon as they left, a dog - this one had a thinning, hazel coat - peeked out of the woods. I walked in its direction, and it stepped into the highway and bounced from one paw to the next, almost like it was dancing. It winked, threw its head back and let out one bellering howl, then vanished back into the woods.

FOG

I love the fog.

It makes the world feel intimate and less real.

And a little magical, too.

It makes me feel like I'm driving through some dreary version of Narnia that was taken over by the grey queen instead of the white, and I belong there just like the guy with the annoying silver headlights behind me that are thankfully muffled enough by the fog that I can still see.

Yes. Muffled. Sometimes words don't have to be used in the exactly correct way because those lights are so loud my eyes have to cover their ears.

Why do I have to go to work? I just want to sit in my car, in the fog, and feel intimate and slightly creeped out at the same time.

I want to sit at home and search for patterns on my ceiling, because it reminds me of being a kid, those patterns in the plaster popcorn.

Lions, tigers, bears, and naked women. Nice. Oh, but
don't forget the demons.

Even with the demons, being a kid was a better time,
because no matter how many times my mother
lost all of our money or scattered part of my face
across the seat of a car, or drove so fast I thought
we'd wreck, I still knew she loved me and would
take care of me.

"Maybe I'll just wrap this fucking car around a tree
and put us both out of our misery."

I knew she loved me even when my handprint-
bruised arms ached while I cried into my freshly
laundered pillow.

I knew she'd take care of me even when we had no
money but she gave some of that zero to a man
who was just taking advantage of her.

Fifteen minutes later, I realize I'm sitting in the gym
parking lot, and the fog is not so close any more.

The harshness of the world is just day-to-day life. I
should pick myself up by my boot straps, drink
more water, make sure I don't miss my doctor and
therapy appointments, and not eat carbs.

How can I do any of that when I was taught as a child
that bad feelings go away with a trip to
McDonalds? That a ten piece, large fries, a Big
Mac, and a chicken fajita (McDonald's used to
have those, look it up...) are an acceptable meal
size for one person. Don't forget that large Coke.
Thanks.

Mmm. Taste of diabetes.

Then, when the bullies called me fat, I wondered if
my mother was wrong. Nah, she couldn't be. I

was just worthless, and I was doing something
wrong.

Shut up, Cody. Try not to exist too loudly.

Fade into the fog, into the realm of the Grey Witch.
Maybe she's beautiful and terrible, and maybe
she'll love you.

But, probably not, because you talk too much, you're
too fat. Get into the gym, the sun is coming up and
burning the fog away.

No Grey Witch. Only one headphone. Alone.

THE SOUND OF SILENCE

Safina stumbled and took her fall into a shoulder roll. The cobblestone planter, made from the same red stones this part of the mall was, sprayed into her face as the top half of it shattered. A ripple that looked like heat-sheen had caught the top, where Safina's head would have been, if not for her loss of footing. She leapt to her left again, flinging a couple of potshot fireballs with the two auto-wands that had been her grandfather's.

She found herself at the front of an old movie theatre, and ducked behind a chunky 1970's Earth-esque pillar. That was when this part of the mall had been built, and likely by Earthpeople of some sort. It just made sense, due to the architecture.

Another wave came, and knocked some plaster from the pillar, showing the rebar skeleton underneath. Definitely Earth work. The masons of her homeland, Cyndwyll, didn't make hollow pillars. It made no sense.

Safina kicked off the pillar, firing two concussive blasts at it, one from each of her autowands. She was propelled backwards, just short of a bathroom stall she'd been trying for. She needed a mirror, and hers was broken during the first ambush from the backlanders, over by the creepy room with all of the naked mannequins. She gestured to the door, it wasn't locked, so it opened easily, thank the Creator. She wasn't an opener, she was just Mall Security. Still prestigious, but not many of the Mall Corps Officers were openers. That was left to the Basement People, and the Ways.

She slid through the door as it opened, slammed it and locked it as she stood. That she could do, because there was a deadbolt. She pulled a small orb from her pocket, and popped it open like a coin-machine egg. The orb halves gleamed ebony in the light that was released. The small light sprite wheeled about her head, giggling tinnily. She smiled.

She loved the sprites. They were from her homeland, and they reminded her forcibly of summer nights, running naked through the forests, and stolen kisses. Her grey-blue skin prickled with goosepimples at the thought. Why was she being so whimsical? The yellow hairs on the back of her head and neck crackled to life.

They were close now. A concussion shook the door, spraying dust in through the edges.

"Stupid, Saff," she muttered to herself, in the language of the Mea Mall People. "Kixj diewcwe," she whispered in Cyndwyllli, aiming her left autowand. An orange light oozed around the edges of the door, leaving behind a dark, smooth substance, much like the ore the Sprite Orb was made of. The Cyndwylli were known, mostly, for their architecture. Though Safina's family was mostly military or law enforcement of some kind (She had eight cousins, three siblings, four aunts, and three uncles that were also in the Mall Corps.), all Cyndwylli are trained, starting in primary school, to make; to repair, build, and refine. She had no time, now, to admire her handiwork.

She rushed to a mirror, drew the much-practiced circle with her hand, and said, "Corps HQ, this is Corporal Syrfveli. Unit Wufgr dash Bubwe stroke Marmalade, calling from—" she checked a half-orb crystal attached to her wrist, it spoke directly into her mind, feeding her the information she needed, "Sector Pelican dash Orpheo dot Tygon. Quadrant Thirteen dash Brixen dash Ho'oeo."

A face swam into view in the mirror. Slightly leonid, male, his green mane expertly coiffed, his uniform much less rumpled than Safina's, and not covered by a Cyndwilli Bolng-leather frock coat. His orange eyes sparkled with humor. "Saff, are you supposed to be in the backlands?"

"Yes, Kwitan. I am on a mission for the Chief Inspector. There is a group of the Pard that have been harassing the few merchants that use this way to get to the Brixen door. There's talk of a Sound Siphon"

"Oooh. Gotta stop that. I thought all of the Sound Siphons had been rounded up. Plus, those Brixens make killer venison jerky. Can't have that supply being shut off."

"Yes, not to mention, you know, the cure for every autoimmune disease from AIDS to the Cormo'a Plague comes from Brixen," a loud blast, and the whole room shuddered.

"Oh, they sound like they're right on top of you." Kwitan chuffed.

"Yes, they are. There's no other exit. I'm trapped."

"I don't know if I can get an opener down there, fast enough. One of the banking districts is between here and there, and you know about their anti-porting policies. Might take days. Did you bring any rati— wait. Saff. You're a Cyndwilli. Make a door!"

Safina's heart sank. "Kwi, you know what that entails, right? You know how angry that can make the Mall, how many magics can be involved. What about the Vroobles?" She glanced over at a bit of writing on the wall. *Long Die the Prince* it said, then below that, in what looked like the scorch marks of a hex, *And may his Pard choke on his blood. Build a bridge.* "Don't answer that, Kwi. I've got this."

"Just tell the Vroobles. Make a small door," Safina walked away from the mirror as Kwitan spoke, "Saff? Saff?! What are you gonn—" Safina waved the magic away, and the mirror returned to being just a mirror, which is still pretty significant.

"C'mon, Saff," she said to herself. "Just think," a beat, " Vroobles first." Another shockwave rocked the door. Safina aimed her left wand, again, at the door. "Dierudt ybvewljlvke."

A mesh of the same shiny, obsidian colored substance spread from Safina's wand, covering the door in a web of the stuff. Even if the door went, this would offer some protection. Safina drew in a deep breath, aiming the left wand at the wall opposite the door, between the mirrors and the first stall.

"Vroobles. Warn the Vroobles, first," She couldn't think like this, she was going to make a stupid mistake. She massaged the bridge of her nose.

She pointed the left wand at the wall, "Awolelrw rubt," she spoke at the wall. A hole, about an inch square, opened into the wall, through the inner supports, and to a narrow strip of what looked like model train landscape, a darkened hillside, specifically.

She heard tiny alarms going off, and an amplified voice, "All patching squads to the South Wall, we have damage. May the Creator help us, it's those backlanders again!"

She put her lips up to the opening in the wall, "Esteemed Vrooblery, most important Master Vrooble, can you hear my voice?" Another blast to the door. The room shook, again.

"Yes, we can hear you. Are you responsible for these terrible wallquakes, backlander?" The amplified voice answered back.

"Indirectly. Members of the Pretending Prince's Pard are chasing me, I am not one of their number, I am an officer of the Mall Corps" More concussions, successive now, "and I need to pass through this wall."

"You know the danger involved? If you make a portal just small enough to crawl through, and low on the wall, it will affect us the least. The Mall may not like it, or even allow it if you aren't an opener. It would take a Cyndwylli Maker Mage to even begin to think of it," The voice sounded confused, toward the end. "Come to think of it, how did you punch a hole in our wall?" Said the Head Vrooblery, "There's strongest magics there!"

"Actually, I am Cyndwylli. I'm also in a bit of a hurry. I have to get somewhere, regardless, or, rather, in regard of the Pard," Safina said, another barrage shaking the room.

"Well, then, aim low and remember that we are here," Said the Vrooblery, "Please."

"Of course, esteemed Vrooblery," Safina said, training her left-hand wand on the lower third of the wall, "Nljw xelqkaolxw," she spoke at the wall. A hole, just big enough for her to get through opened up, and began to close immediately. She wiggled through, barely getting her ankle out before the hole closed, as if it had never been there. A shiver ran through the masonry, and Safina knew the Mall was angry. She could still faintly hear the Vrooble sirens inside the wall.

Safina immediately pulled a pair of goggles down from her saffron yellow hairline. She pushed back the soft leather frock coat, and holstered her autowands, the right one on her left hip, the left one on the right side of her ribcage. She spun the lenses of her goggles, and said, "Illumination, eighty-five percent." What met her eyes, both dazzled and feared her, at once. Huge decorations for Yuletide and Erframinster Festivals were piled about. Those creepy seventies and eighties Earth mall animatronics, along with the otherworldly spires and helices that made up the sentient decorations of the Eframin, all seemingly in torpor, now. One cabinet in the corner, quite wide and twice as tall, seemed to resonate with magic. Its aura danced and shimmered in her goggles, and it put pictures of snorting breath and running through a snowy wood into her head. It creeped Safina out, and she shook her head to clear it. She'd heard stories of beings actually worshipping these things, Earther and Erframin alike. She couldn't seem to stop watching them, for fear they would spring to life and eat her, as some sacrifice. She had seen an Earth film, once, wherein deer like the ones represented here became angry, and turned on Earth humans. She shook her head as flecks of dust and debris crumbled from the ceiling with the latest barrages on the room behind her.

A loud shudder and crack meant the Backlanders had broken through the door in the bathroom behind her. She looked around for an exit. She noticed, to her left, a large sheet of tar paper. There was a very good chance that, behind this tar paper was a security grate covering a large opening into the mall corridor. She cleared the few feet, keeping a wary eye on the decorations piled against the far wall.

"Stop being a baby, Safina," she said to herself, shaking her head once more. She tore back the tar paper, and was heartened when she saw the grate she expected, and the empty corridor beyond. She pulled at the grate, but it didn't budge. She looked toward the bottom of the metal latticework, and found the lock. She pointed her left autowand at the lock.

"Ybnljw," she whispered, and the lock fell apart. She wasn't an opener, but she might be a maker-mage yet. Safina lifted the grate just enough to slide under, and broke into a run as soon as she found her feet.

————

Safina didn't stop to catch her breath until she had rounded six corners, and bolted down two flights of stairs. She was still in the backlands, but not as deep. There were still viable shops in this area, though the Brixen Gate was still the closest World Door, and Brixen station still the closest stop for The Train. Both behind her, deeper into enemy territory.

She stepped out of the stairwell, quietly sealing the door behind her with Cyndwilli grout. She felt a bit bad doing this, knowing it would make life harder on the next person to use this stairwell, but knew it would buy her time if the Pard brought out hounds, if they had hounds. Likely they had rift cats, like the black one that always stalked at the Prince's side in the stories Brixen parents told to scare small children. Safina shuddered at the thought, and surveyed her surroundings.

The stairwell opened on a rundown square of shops, nestled in an arm of connecting corridors. One of the corridors was large, and seemed to be a tributary to one of the main corridors, likely the Cor-Brixen, the main artery from Cor Morsheth's Court, near the banking district, to the Brixen gate.

Cor Morsheth and his Nightmare Court were the last line of defense for the bankers, against the Prince and his Pard. If Saf could find this Sound Siphon everyone was talking about, before the backlanders, and get it to the Nightmare Court, Cor Morsheth could keep it safe. The Prince feared The Courts of Night. The Night Queen had given orders that the Prince be thrown into the Midnight without a trial.

As all of this rushed through Safina's mind, she looked to her right, through to the opposite end of the square of shops, bedotted here and there, by children's coin-operated ride-ons, a couple of claw machines and a handful of tables. The corridor that led away in that direction was much smaller than its opposer, and turned a sharp corner to the west, off toward the deeper Backlands. Safina would look for a place to rest and eat, and she would keep an eye on that thoroughfare, particularly.

Safina's stomach grumbled in agreement to this sentiment, and her nose led her to a small stand that sold battered, deep-fried meat on sticks that reminded her of corn dogs, except the meat was more fragrant and spiced, and the batter looked to have more bite. She ordered two of the savory confections, which the Brixen male who took her money called 'Shipsticks'. She also ordered a basket of fried vegetables that tasted to Saf like a cross between turnips and potatoes, very reminiscent of her homeworld's tuber, the fyveiir. She chewed one of the shoestring-cut vegetables as she tried to pay. The Brixen smiled, and refused her currency.

"If you don't accept Mea currency, I have gold," Saf said as she fumbled at the pouches on her belt.

"Make sense, m'dear lawkeeper. Yew protect us from the Backlanders an' all. We be grateful. T'would be an insult o'both sides for us to take yer gold. Sit in peace and nourish yerself. Have some grog," the vendor said, the Brixen seafaring accent thick, and very reminiscent of a stereotypical hollywood pirate.

"Oh, no. I can't drink on duty," Saf said, putting up a hand.

"Ah, but this be the Fire of Covfe! It shan't make ye inheebreeated, t'will give ye courage," the vendor said with a smile that made light dance in his eyes.

Safina took the mug, raised it in thanks, and headed for the tables arranged in front of the small stand. She sat, sipped at the Covfe, and felt it burn all the way down. The burn was almost comforting. She smiled and took another, larger pull from the mug. This proved to be a mistake, as the first sip, just then, hit her stomach. She belched loudly, expelling blue flames.

"Good, innit?" The Brixen shopkeeper hollered across to her, as the few patrons milling about applauded uproariously.

Safina raised her glass and answered with a feeble, "Sure is."

She kept a wary eye out, now that she'd made a spectacle, and bit into the shipstick almost absentmindedly. Her mind was snapped out of its absence by the utter astonishment of her taste buds.

Her eyes widened and she couldn't help but smile as she

took a second huge bite of the juicy, tender, perfectly spiced meat. Clear juices from the center dribbled down her chin as she chewed, and the usually demure Cyndwilli hadn't care one. She took a swig of the Covfe, and it only heightened the flavor of the meat. She shoveled the fries into her mouth, and downed the second meat skewer in record time. When finished, she wiped her mouth, and belched a three-foot wide fireball. She stood, walked back to the stand, plunked a gold piece down on the counter, and waved away the Brixen shopkeeper as he began to protest.

"It is a tip, I insist. That is the best fare I've eaten at a food stand in a decade, and I do feel much better for having drank of your brew. Thank you."

The shopkeeper bowed, thanked her, and Saf headed off with newfound resolve. She was going to check the shops for a new two-way mirror before heading back into the deeper backlands.

———

She found one, in the first shop she happened upon. It was second hand, but, according to the shabby-looking lady with the cotton-bud hair sitting behind a circle of glass cases, it had been thoroughly disenchanted, and was ready for any use. Of course Safina had to ask that she be allowed to check it before buying it, and the Lady of the Cases obliged.

"Anyfing for m'lady of the law," she smiled widely, that same light dancing in her eyes as the food stand vendor. They must really value the Corps here, Saf thought. She smiled as she lowered her goggles, and turned the dials around the lenses.

"Detect magic," Safina said as she held the smallish, leather-encased mirror up to the light. The mirror shone with a faint bluish white light, meaning only that it was ready to be re-enchanted. Safina nodded. "I'll take it. Ho—" Safina stopped mid sentence. Her goggles were still on, and still set to detect magic. She let out a strangled gasp as she noticed, on a shelf in one of the shop's windows, a roiling ball of darkness, then light, blotting out anything around it for a full six inches. She pushed the goggles up her forehead, and kept her eyes on the spot.

What appeared in the space of the twisting cloud of blackness-and-light was a small jewelry box, topped by a red-breasted robin, his head thrown back in frozen-yet-jubilant song. Looking at it caused Safina to shiver to her soul. She walked over to it, and picked it up.

"Find somefing else ye fancy, dearie?" Said the shopkeeper, causing Safina to jump.

"N-no—umm—I mean, yes. Very much," Saf steeled herself, so as to not let on what she thought this object to be, "M-my mother. She loves trinket boxes. She also is fond of songbirds," Safina said as she laid both the box and the mirror on the glass case in front of the crone-like shopkeeper. The shopkeeper pushed her bottle-bottom spectacles down her nose and surveyed the two items.

"Ugh. That box always give me the creeping terror," The old lady said. "Glad to be rid o't."

"How much for them both, madam?" Said Saf.

"Ah, for one as beautiful as thee," The shopkeeper reached out with a gnarled, arthritic hand and rubbed the curve of Safina's jaw, "Nuffing but the grace you've afforded me shop by spending time in," she smiled, again, with the dancing light in her eyes.

"Nonsense," Safina said, laying a gold and silver piece on the case.

"I must insist that no member of the Co—" The shopkeeper was cut off by Safina.

"I appreciate it very much, and still consider this a discount. Thank you," Safina scooped up the two items, shoving the robin-box into a pouch at her right hip, and extracting an autowand from a holster at the same hip. She began to gesture at the mirror with the wand as she walked out of the shop, trying not to hurry.

———

As Safina exited the shop, she looked around for a place that would give a semblance of privacy. She saw a deep alcove at the entrance of a seemingly closed shop. She headed for it, glancing at the patrons scattered about the place. Patrons that nodded and smiled as she crossed to the alcove. She pulled her hood halfway up, thought that would make her look more suspect, and dropped it back to rest behind her neck. She huddled into the alcove and spoke to the newly enchanted mirror.

"Corps HQ, this is Corporal Syrfveli. Unit Wufgr dash Bubwe stroke Marmalade, calling from Sector Stoogent dot Pelicula dash panthro. Quadrant Nine dash Cor dash Brixen"

The mirror's face swam and the face of Kwitan came into view.

"Thank Farbarr," Kwitan said, "We were about to call your brother."

"I'm fine. I got away. I stopped to eat and catch my

breath, and to buy a new two-way. I think I found something." Saf whispered.

"What? Why are you whispering?" Kwitan said, in full voice. A couple of people sitting at the Shipstick Stand's little clutch of tables glanced her way. Safina smiled and nodded. They went back to what they were doing, both smiling benignly. It seemed all of the other patrons had went into shops or moved on, and the Shipstick Stand had lowered a large wooden shutter over its front. Safina cursed herself for being oblivious enough not to notice this sooner.

"Because I'm trying not to make a huge spectacle of myself. I'd like to come home, someday, in one, me-shaped piece." Saf whisper-barked at the mirror.

"Oh," Kwitan said, now whispering, too, "Sorry, I didn't think. Dispatchers don't see a lot of field work."

"You're forgiven. I need you to get Ro Qallatrix, like, five minutes ago."

"Regent Qallatrix? Like, the seven-thousand year old Rekchäan sorcerer? Are you dead mental?" Kwi was yelling now. The two eaters from the small food court snapped their heads back to face Safina, again.

"Just some official business," Saf said to the eaters. "Sorry for any inconvenience. My dispatcher gets very excited over new places, and he's never been to your wing before," Saffina smiled as convincingly as she could and turned back to the two-way mirror. "By The Great Architect, you are going to get me well and truly dead if you don't control the volume of your face-vent."

"Sorry, but you really want me to bother an ancient dark sorcerer?" Kwi said, visibly shaking at the thought.

"No, Kwi, I want you to order me some doughnuts," She said, then whisper-yelling, continued, "Yes I want you to bother him. I think I found a Sound Siphon," Saf regretted her words the moment she spoke.

The two eaters tossed off their tattered looking cloaks, revealing themselves as Pard members, one by his leopard-print frock-coat, the other by his long leather jacket with a snarling black panther on the back. Each had various scarves and bits of fabric tied about their middles and limbs that were of various leopard prints. They both Brixen, judging by the dark eyes, sun-tanned skin, and altogether privateer look, though that look seemed to have passed through the lens of a cheesy 80s action film.

"I knew they were too nice! Kwi, get the Regent and call me back, I'll try to get somewhere safe," Saf said as she passed a hand over the mirror.

"Just leave the two-way on so I—" Kwitan managed to squawk as the mirror went blank and Saf stuffed it into a pouch. In the same motion, she drew her autowands. A voice from behind her caused her to fairly leap backwards.

"We hoped one of yours'd find it fer us, dearie," The old woman from the knick-knack shop said with a greasy smile. A leopard-print shawl now draped about her slight shoulders, "We ain't versed in that type-o magic, ya see. We's simple folk, and the master wants all of those little baubles somethin' awful. We're f'ankful for yer help, shame we have to tear thee to pieces, now."

As she was talking, a pair of huge, bright red rift cats, striped like tigers, had stalked out of the old woman's shop, "These be me brothers. They displeased the master, and this is the price ye pay fer that. They do 'is bidding now, wif' little question. Don'ya, boys?"

The largest of the cats rubbed his head against the old

woman's shoulder, and she raised a hand to scratch his ear. Both cats chuffed, pulling their lips back from their teeth.

Safina pointed both autowands to the ceiling, muttered a spell, turned, and bolted down the sharply bending corridor that led deeper into the backlands to the West. The ceiling unmade itself as Safina turned, bricks and dust tumbling down on the woman and her cat-brothers. The spells from the two in the food court hit just a foot shy of Saf's retreating heels.

What did she mean, Saffina thought, *those were her brothers? Can the Prince transfigure People? Surely not.*

Safina cleared the length of two football fields before she heard growlings behind her, apologized to the Mall, and muttered the same spell as before, aiming an autowand at the ceiling, and one at the wall, "Swnikuah," she said with conviction. The Mall audibly groaned as bricks, mortar, dust, and concrete rained and flowed. Safina ran on.

"I'd better call back to HQ," She said to herself, as she ran, pulling the two-way from her pouch and holstering an autowand. "Corps HQ, this is Corporal Syrfveli. Unit Wufgr dash Bubwe stroke Marmalade, calling from Sector Stoogent dot Pelicula dash panthro. Quadrant... I don't know what quadrant. Just get me Kwitan, dammit. I'm running for my life."

She saw a door ahead, it looked like a service closet. Just then, she heard a distant bellow from one of the cats, so she dashed into the door, sealing it behind her. She prayed there'd be no more holiday decorations. Mercifully, it was a broom closet.

Her mirror blinked to life as she turned back to it, for all of the above happened in three rushed seconds. She cast a final spell at the door as Kwitan spoke.

"What the Rekshä happened? Oh, sorry Master Regent... I.. Uh... No offense meant, sir. Umm, Saf?"

"I'm here, Kwi." Saf said moving her face back into frame of the two-way, and noticing a figure that seemed to be made of living smoke, with a glowing edge of yellowish-green, stood behind and to the left of Kwitan, "Master Regent. It is good to see you," Saf said.

"Doubtful. What is your business with me. This one spoke of a Sound Siphon." Said the Master Regent, matter-of-fact.

Safina produced the robin-box after a bit of fumbling, and held it up to the mirror.

"Sweet Amarose," the Master Regent exclaimed, as much as the Shadow Däan ever do, "I know it. It was enchanted in Earth's English Restoration Era. It was used to silence true witches. It did more damage than The Hammer, on that planet. You must get it to the closest Regent to you. That is —" he was cut off by Safina.

"Cor Morsheth. I'll get it there. Thank you, Master Regent." Safina wasted no time. She waved the mirror off, replaced it and the robin-box in their pouches, then bolted out the door, back the way she'd come. She would have to fight.

By the time she neared the obstacle she'd created, the rift cats and backlanders had broken through. The cats sprinted toward her halfway to her engineered cave-in, and she sprinted toward them. This confused them, and caused them to hesitate. She drew her autowands, and pointed one each at the large cats. "Wbrinv," she exclaimed. The floor seemed to rise up as the two cats were surrounded by flowing cyclopean slabs.

Safina asked herself why she hadn't done that earlier,

and realized it is hard to build tombs while firing spells over your shoulder. Emboldened by pride in herself, she lept to the top of, and over, one of the small tombs, and didn't miss a step sprinting back toward the wing in which she'd first met these foes.

Not far down the corridor, she met the old woman, riding along on a leopard-skin carpet that hovered at an average man's running speed. The two other backlanders were hot on the old woman's rug-dust.

Thinking on her feet, Saf muttered "Restraints," pointing autowands to each side of the old woman, at the other two. The spell she'd learned in Mea Corps Academy worked like it always did, and glittery silver ropes of energy snaked around both of the backlanders, binding them hand and foot. They both faceplanted.

Safina couldn't help but chuckle. As she did, using her momentum, she lay back and slid deftly under the old woman's carpet. She stood on the other side, and muttered the same spell at the old woman and her carpet. They fell to the floor with a soft thud. Safina smiled over her shoulder, proud of herself. As she turned back the direction she'd been running, all she heard was a soft *whoosh*, and the world went dark.

––––––––

When she awoke, Safina was not bound, but she found her autowands, and the pouches containing her two-way mirror and robin-box gone. She jumped to her feet, and realized she was on a ledge overlooking the canals, deep in the backlands. A voice boomed from behind her, though it seemed to be barely above whispering, too.

"Sit, girl," The voice said. Safina sat, indeed. Hard. "Now, face me," the voice commanded, and Safina turned on her butt.

The sight that met her eyes was that of pure nightmare for anyone who knew of the backlands, anyone who had grown up hearing the stories. Sitting on a stone throne, spread with furs of various types, was a large, beautiful male Person. He was definitely Brixen. His features were sharp, his almond eyes dark and sharp as obsidian in his tanned face. His dark hair was pulled into a tight knot at the base of his head, and was as deep as the Midnight. He wore a white blouse, laced but not tied, and loose-fitting, dark purple silk pants. Binding his middle was a red sash. He carried no weapon that could be seen, but spun Safina's right autowand in his hand, lazily. At his right lay a rift cat that managed to be blacker than the man's hair.

"Pick up your jaw, girl. It is unseemly to gawp," He smiled brilliantly. Safina knew why people would follow this man, even love him. "Have anything to tell me about this trinket of yours?" He made a deft sleight-of-hand motion, and the robin-box appeared in his left palm.

And the words of the prophets are written on the bathroom stalls —

"I-It's just a p-present. F-f-for my mother. She loves t-trinket boxes and son—"

—and corridor walls —

"Hmmph," The man said, and the black rift cat simply appeared on top of Safina, drooling and snarling into her face. "You must be lying. Lying makes my cat angry. Do you know who I am, girl? Say it, if you do."

"Y-you're the P-Pretending P-prince of the Backlands."

Safina swallowed hard, trying not to vomit at the stench of the creature's breath.

—and whispered in the sound—

"Just wanted to hear you say it. Eat, my beauty." As he said the words, the black rift cat tore Safina's face from her skull, and she screamed until it bit her vocal cords from her throat. The canals fell silent once again as the cat ate quietly, and the Prince turned his new treasure over in his hand.

—of silence.

I DON'T BELIEVE

I don't believe in poets,
They don't exist here for me
The beauty of the sunrise
Is more than any of us can see
I don't believe in lovers
Or their entreaty at first sight
I don't believe in angels
That are made only of light
I don't believe in kindness
Or that most have some to spare
I don't believe in decency
Or a person's will to care
I don't believe in starlight
Or the wonder of the sky
I don't believe in striving
Or the endless need to try
I don't believe in money
Or material wealth and greed
I don't believe in body

Or if I'm cut that I will bleed
I don't believe in summer
Or winter's icy pall
I don't believe in urbanity
Or the wilds unending call
I don't believe in anything
Today is a bad day
Tomorrow is another
Maybe it won't be this way
But for today, if you see me
Don't speak on hopes golden glow
Sometimes we must be somber
And allow our gloom to show
It's the exhalation of our soul breath
A time to scrape the rock
It's the eternal loping backswing
The tick to our heart's tock
Don't hate the days you hate things
Hold them dear and near at heart
Because without the bad days
There'd be no fresh new start
Tomorrow I'll believe again
In love and joy and life
Today allow my heart to live
In pain and toil and toil and strife
Positivity is great and all
But don't say negativity's not real
Don't be a thief of validity
Let people feel how they must feel.

THE DANCERS IN THE DESERT

The Commandant was silhouetted against the setting sun, the horizon crowded by the larger shapes of the half-shadowed colossi. The Dancers of the Desert had stood at the entrance to this waste for at least three hundred years. They had been raised during the rule of Lurean the Cyano-magus, and people were still terrified of them. Heat shimmer gave them a vague sense of movement, and the unmoving Commandant fought off an involuntary shudder.

She tossed a chewed-up cigaro to the ground and addressed her lug, an indentured member of the trash-class, tasked with carrying the Commandant's gear, "You believe these stories, lug?"

"N-no, ma'am. They are f-faerie stories made to scare children from wandering into the wastes, ma'am." The lug, whose name was Tuskrat, but whose friends just called him "Tusk" or "Rat". Most called him "Fatrat", though, because he had few friends, and was fat. The Commandant just called him "lug" or "coward", or some colorful variation of the two.

"Don't lie to me, you sniveling craven. Do you believe the stories?" The Commandant looked over her shoulder. The strange beauty of her hard face caused Tuskrat's breath to catch in his throat.

"Yes. I do, ma'am. Not a generation ago, someone tried to pass this way, and his passing angered the Dancers." With a huge gulp, Tuskrat went silent, wordlessly praying that the Commandant would not press him for further detail.

"And?" The Commandant waited for a long moment, head still turned, impatience radiating. "Speak the rest of the story, lug, or I will remove your exosuit and make you walk the first day with no water."

"I'd not survive, honored Commandant!" The big man said with a note of panic in his voice.

"That is the point of a threat, lug," The Commandant turned away, refastening her respirator mask against the blowing sands, now done with her smoke, "Now, speak," She said, facing the blaze of the setting sun.

"Th-the Dancers tore him apart, painting their stone bodies with his f-fluids, and adorning themselves with his bones. Their l-laughing and whooping could be heard as far back as Hanmarole City. H-his screams could, too."

There were many bones adorning the bodies and sandstone clothes of the colossi, and their brightly colored paint was faded, but the red was noticeably less so, even from a distance. The Commandant laughed. A sharp, dry sound, "Your silly, caitiff stories amuse me, lug. We will stop for rest the first time you begin to weep, as my thanks for the entertainment." The Commandant strode, unafraid into the desert, toward the huge coryphée effigies.

Tuskrat followed, his fear-quakes hidden by the clunky

exo-suit that was pushed through his flesh, and welded to his bones.

———

Though the Dancers looked close from the edge of town, where the two travelers had their previous discussion, the first pair, flanking the hard-packed path in to the Amamenshee Waste, were nearly a half mile out of town. They had trod the straight foot-road all the way there, as the enchantments and under-structure of the it were the only things that kept the sandmaws from pulling a traveler under the shifting sand. The only way to their destination lay before them, between the giant sandstone revelers.

The Commandant didn't falter for half a heart-tick. With no perceived hesitation, her boots crunched on the ancient thoroughfare between the first two dancers. The wind died, and the desert went silent.

The statues were dressed as contemporary gauchos would be, on Earth. Wide brimmed hats, shirts with intricate patterns, a few with ornamented ponchos that had once been boldly, colorfully painted, bolo ties, straight-legged pants, and high-heeled boots. They were frozen in various dance poses, a dance that seemed energetic, hands still-clapping, like a suspended Brazilian Earther Catira dance. Their faces were grotesque, twisted into macabre smiles and expressions of terrible joy, everything exaggerated. Skulls were set into many of the indentations that made up the pupils of their eyes. The details of all of these features were smoothed by three centuries of sandstorms, but not as much as you might think, much like the pressed sand path between them. In the near distance, sandmaws rose and fell, stopping sometimes in their dives, to silently and hungrily stare at the travelers.

The Commandant picked up all of this as she passed the first two figures, never slowing, brazenly staring into the skull-pupiled eyes. As the first pair fell out of her periphery, there was a grinding sound, and a sizeable quantity of sand fell from one of the statues.

Tuskrat made a pathetic, small choking sound and froze, his exo-suit lurching a bit, before painfully forcing his body forward.

The Commandant loosened and removed her respirator. "Pull it in, lug. It was simply the desert wind. Don't be a weanling," The Commandant said, sliding a hand under her heavy desert cloak, to the hilt of her regulation searsaber. She silently flicked a switch on the power box perched at her hip, allowing the sword's heating element to start up. There was no wind, the desert was as still as a grave, save the near-silent comings and goings of the 'maws. She sped up her pace.

Tuskrat swallowed hard. Many thought him a dullard, but he was just quiet. His observational skills were far above average, especially in the desert he'd grown up in. He had seen the colossus move. He had also seen the Commandant power up her sword. He tightened the straps on the two large packs he carried, and spun his heavy rifle from its resting place on his shoulder blade, down to patrol carry position. The Commandant either didn't notice, or didn't care. Her eyes were scanning the next set of statues. They were halfway through the broken hall the twelve stone giants made when the Commandant decided to speak.

"What a bunch of hornlunk scat," The Commandant spat, "These unmoving hunks of compressed sand coming to life and doing anything is about as—" The Commandant was cut off by a scream, rifle fire, and a loud roar. The scream and rifle fire had come from behind her, the roar from her left. Her boots ground into a fighting stance, the screaming hot blade in front of her. The golem that had tried to grab her recovered from Tuskrats attack and reached down for her with its undamaged hand, as Tuskrat fired on its dancing partner. The thundering that arose from the ground as the other effigies began to dance brought madness and terror up with it.

The statue that Tuskrat had first wounded had its other hand sheered off by a quick underhand blow, the descalescent ore blade passing through the sandstone like butter. The statues closed into a circle as they danced, blocking the gaps before and after Tuskrat and the Commandant.

"We have to get outside of them. They'll crush us!" Tuskrat said, leaping backward to avoid a huge boot heel.

"Without question, lug. How do you propose we do that? Duck between them and risk tumbling off the path into the stomach of a 'maw?" The Commandant said, parrying a giant foot, herself, lopping it off at the ankle with an arching swing.

"Blast a leg off the one blocking our route, and make a dash." Tuskrat said.

"You first." The Commandant answered.

Tuskrat twiddled a dial on his rifle, aimed at the hip of the Dancer blocking the smooth road, and squeezed the trigger. A blast of red energy two feet wide splashed from the muzzle of his weapon. The leg was mostly vaporized, and he made a mad dash for the gap it left, pushing his exo-suit to its limits.

Before he was a foot from the gap, with unbelievable speed, the leg reformed and kicked him sprawling into the dancer opposite it. That dancer aimed a stomping sole for his head, but he rolled away in time.

"Good show, lug," The Commandant said, "I had a theory that would happen, based on the reforming of the first hand you blew off."

"Y-you almost let me die to test a theory." Tuskrat said, obliquely, eyes wide.

"Town is a meer half mile away, and lugs are cheap." The Commandant shrugged, sidestepping another stomp.

Tuskrat, being used to people wishing him ill, shrugged off the affront. "Maybe we reason with them? We don't know their original intent. I panicked."

"Their eyes are literally death's heads, lug. Do you think their intention is a tea party?"

Tuskrat lay his gun on the ground, anyway, then his packs, so as to stand as tall and straight as possible. The dancing continued, but the Dancers no longer tried to stomp him, at least right away.

"Dancers! Please hear me!" Tuskrat began, "We are passing to the Mount of Scales with no harm intended. We only wish to protect what is there!"

The eyes of each dancer turned, and focused on the large man. Stunned, the Commandant turned to him, as well, letting her guard fall.

"We wish you and the Sacred Waste no harm. I know the stories of old, the stories of the desert tribes. I am of their blood." Tuskrat pulled aside one lapel of his sweat-soaked, roughspun shirt, pulling two bone buttons free from their buttonholes as he did.

Covering Tuskrat's chest was a beautiful, colorful tribal

tattoo, with markings that resembled those on the clothing of the Dancers. On his left pectoral, a large rat with oversized tusks was represented in bright blues, pinks, and ochres. It stood out from Tuskrat's olive skin like bright blue text on a dark computer screen. The Commandant flexed the muscles in her jaw.

"What are you doing, lug?" The Commandant groaned.

"Saving our hides." Tuskrat spat over his shoulder, with uncharacteristic conviction. He turned back to the Dancers, "Let us pass, and I personally vow I will not let any harm come to our sacred lands." The dancing stopped, suddenly.

"This you vow on your life, Honored Rat?" The Dancer facing Tuskrat said.

The Commandant's jaw dropped, possibly for the first time in her life, "Honored Rat?" she laughed, "What kind of nonsense is that? What is hono—"

"SILENCE!" The Dancer addressing Tuskrat boomed. "Do not speak amongst us, imperialist scum. Do not dishonor this Child of Dust any further."

With a disgusted eyeroll, the Commandant complied.

"This is my friend and employer, Great Dancer. She is here to help me protect our ways of life, and restore honor to the Dustlands."

The Dancer regarded the Commandant. "She wears the uniform of the imperialists."

"Indeed, Avatar of Moklauchee, but she is not like the rest. She is kind, and caring. She lets me rest when the cursed metal they have pushed into my guts causes me hurt. She gives me food, water, and medicine. She is not cruel like the rest." Tuskrat lied.

"Though you lie about her nature, we will let you pass because of the selfless love you have shown to her, not because of any merit of her own." The Dancer said, stepping aside.

"I am sorry it took me a time to know you, Dancers. Fear clouded my mind."

"Fear and a lapse in reverence for your own culture, Honored Rat. I hope this doesn't happen again." The dancer replied.

"Never, never again, Guardians of Dust." Tuskrat replied.

"You," The Dancer began, turning its gaze back to the Commandant. "You must learn the error of your ways. You must learn to value others, and truly be kind."

"Weak. Be weak, is what you mean." The Commandant snarled. Before the period fell into place in her sentence, the dancer had scooped her up into a vice-like hand.

The Dancer squeezed, and all of the dancers spoke with one roaring eldritch voice, "Do we appear weak?! We are showing kindness by not adorning ourselves with your parts! Do you speak to us of weakness?!"

For the first time since childhood nightmares, the Commandant was truly scared. "N-no," She said, sounding much like Tuskrat.

"Good. Kindness is not weakness. In caring one may find the greatest strength. Now go. Stick close to your companion, for his kindness is right, and the only thing that saved you, this day."

The Dancer replaced the Commandant on the ground, just high enough from it that she overbalanced and sat down hard. Tuskrat stifled a laugh. The Commandant almost chided him, then thought better of it. The Dancers went back to their original poses, and the desert was silent, again.

Tuskrat bent to pick up the packs, and a breathless Commandant shouldered in, grabbing her pack.

"Commandant, I—"

"You'll nothing. You've saved us both lu— ahh— Tuskrat. You have shown a bravery I have never had, today, while I stood and soiled myself in fear. We will walk through your ancestral lands as equals, or not at all. I could not have done what you have done. My way would have us dead, by now."

"You're welcome." Tuskrat smiled.

"Don't get too full of yourself, you're still a part of this mission, bound by your honor, Honorable Rat." She smiled, a real smile. It was light itself.

In that moment, Tuskrat realized the Commandant was gorgeous. He had always known she was beautiful, but he saw true beauty in her now. He tried to hide his blushing.

The Commandant shouldered her pack and hurried forward. "Come, let us find a place on the path to camp. The exertion has made you quite red-faced, and something, possibly the magic of those Dancers, has made me actually care."

"Care? Commandant, that is awfully close to kindness, even a kind of love!"

"Bite your tongue, lug!" She exclaimed. There was a grinding sound behind her, she jumped, almost unsheathing her sword.

Tuskrat began belly-laughing. After a moment, the Commandant did, too. Their revelry was broken up by a loud alarm emitting from a pouch on the Commandant's belt. She pulled out a palm-sized, hexagonal leather case.

The Commandant opened the case, revealing a mirror of the same shape. The face of a young leonid swam into view, his mane a bit disheveled.

"This is Kwitan of The Mea Mall Corps Central

Headquarters. Have I reached Commandant Aayuun Baclu?" The person in the mirror said.

"Yes. This is the Commandant."

"Have you reached the artifact yet?"

"We have not. We have just endured the trial to pass into the wastes."

"Good. You're closer than we'd hoped. You must hurry. The Pretending Prince has killed one of our number, and stolen a Sound Siphon she had retrieved. You must reach your Siphon before his lot can."

"Don't worry. I have an experienced Native guide, without one, you cannot pass the Guardians. We will head directly to the Mountain. I know my guide knows the way." The Commandant smiled, almost kindly, over to Tuskrat.

"Good. Mea Corps out." The mirror said, then the image dissolved to blankness.

The Commandant pouched the mirror and turned to Tuskrat, who was smiling proudly.

"Oh, don't let it go to your head, lug." The Commandant said, fighting a smile, herself.

"Never!" Tuskrat replied, shouldering his pack and following the Commandant down the road.

HOPE, SOMETIMES

Sometimes there's hope
In the quiet times
When the pain is raging
And the world's lost its rhymes
Sometimes there's hope
In the I-should-be-asleep
And here I lie hoping
Pushing fear down to Deep
Sometimes you revel
And ride out the pain
Closed eyes, breathing carried
A paper boat on a river of rain
Sometimes the rhyme scheme
Flies right off the hype
And your numb hands switch from type to swipe
But some words don't swipe right
So you leave then how they are
Like your words left behind a palpable scar
Flowing inconveniences inconveniences...

Fuck...inconciousness because the word is
"unconsciousness"
And you realize nothing rhymes with
"unconsciousness"
Except for things you know
Like "self-consciousness"
But that's too on the KNOWse
Then you wonder if this poem got away from you
You don't wonder if you should be asleep
You know tomorrow won't go easy on you
But what good is a slumber not deep?
But you'll surrender anyway,
feet dipped in fire
It's almost pleasant now
So close to the wire
You wittily try to end as began
But the phone suddenly won't
Let you scroll up again
So you copy slash paste
In case THIS is THE PIECE
You'll get fortune or fame
Or maybe just some release
Of the tension in your body
The tightness of your yoke
Forcing a last rhyme because
Sometimes. You hope.

THE WAY OF THE WORLD

Their eyes locked, the feelings flowed between them like a river after a rainstorm. She was so beautiful, he thought. Golden hair and sky blue eyes. An angel. He was so beautiful, she thought. Raven hair and blood red eyes. Once an angel. They started toward each other, smooth measured movements, anticipation thick in the air and almost palpable. Their love about to be made known.

Then it happened, like a floodgate had been opened, the ones in white shirts, button down and formal, black pants, sometimes ties. Men women and children poured into the small lobby, shoes making no sound on the white marble floor. They rushed in and stopped behind the golden haired woman, if you could call her that, echoing her slow measured movements. The lobby was large; they were not halfway to each other yet. Once again, as if some release was flipped, movement erupted. The ones in black, ragtag, no two alike, the only thing linking their garments was the consistent black, with the occasional blood red accent. Men women and children poured into the balconies and on top of the reception stand, the receptionist oblivious. The glass in the entrance doors exploded and more poured in, none of the business men scurrying by even noticed, still pushing open the ruined metal skeletons of the glass doors as they came and went. The ones in black paused, coiled, like snakes, or large cats on the prowl, crouched on the balconies or craw-walking in step with the red eyed raven haired man, if you could call him that, echoing his slow calculated movements.

For what seemed like an eternity they came on toward each other in their careful waltz. His red eyes flashed with desire, her blue-white eyes echoed and returned his sentiment. The ones in white organized and trooping behind the woman, rigid and militant. The ones in black crawling down the walls or shambling and gliding along behind the man, venomous and full of cat-calls and curses said in hissing voices under their breath. The white ones completely silent. After a time that cannot be measured in minutes, only in breaths or heart-ticks or the beats of humming bird wing, they were face to face. He lifted a hand to brush a tear from her face. Cacophony erupted. The ones in white flew past the woman, breaking around her and her lover like a rapid around a boulder. The black ones met them, completing the circle around the two. They stared at each other as the battle raged around them. He pulled a dark short sword from the air, it's red blade gleaming with vicious intent. She pulled a large spear, white as driven snow, from the air around her, it's tip gleaming gold and engulfed in flames. They both smiled. A single tear ran down the man's face, her face was already tear stained. In one fluid motion she ran him through with the spear and he, throwing the sword into her chest, burst into flames. She staggered and fell face first into his ashes. What a beautiful dance, she thought as her life-force slipped away.

Their eyes locked, the feelings flowed between them like a river after a rainstorm. She was so beautiful, he thought. Golden hair and sky blue eyes. An angel. He was so beautiful, she thought. Raven hair and blood red eyes. Once an angel. They started toward each other smooth measured movements, anticipation thick in the air and almost palpable. Their love about to be made known.

ANXIETY

Anxiety is a funny little thing
It makes you think the worst of it all
Pulls you along on a funny little string
Leading you to some unnecessary fall
The biting, hot, lukewarm fear
That everything is somehow just wrong
And you know there's really nothing there
It was lying to you all along
But you validate it with thought
Make it real in your mind
Mull over the mundane and frought
Believe all the bad you can find
Sunlight breaks through the clouds
But you realize the daybreak
Is probably just another explosion
Something else you must take
So you fight all you can
Bear what you can bare

Just to see who you were
And why you were there
Then, you sleep.

CHARON'S DAY OFF

"Charon!" the tall thin figure of the cloaked man shouted.

A hunched dark figure in the ferry moored to the bank stirred, then spoke, "Bugger off, if you please, he's having a break!"

Ankou shrugged and looked down at his charge, "Sorry about this," he said "It's never happened before, really a precedent. Hang on." Ankou made a noise as to clear his throat, though his charge was convinced he had none, "Alright then, who in Hell are you?" Ankou's horses tossed their heads and stamped, the old feeble one said to the young strong one, "This should be rich. I didn't know the jobs in the afterlife came with fringe benefits. I wonder if they've started a union?", Now raising his voice to the ferryman, "Oi! Have you lot started a union or sumfink? How much is dues!"

"Do shut up Past, you are scaring our young friend here. I am quite sorry. Now who in Hell are you boatman!"

"Well, as for in Hell, I am known as Naberius," He turned then, showing the appearance of a man sized black crane with flaming red eyes, "but they don't like me much anymore, not after that Johann Weir fellow and his goings on. "Valiant" who ever heard of a "valiant" demon. Anyhow, I had nothing better to do so I told Charon to have a bit of a sit down. You need passage? Acheron this way," He pointed left, "Styx that way," He pointed right, "Though I could have that backwards..."

"You shoulda written it down shouldn't ya!" Yelled Present, the dumber but younger and sturdier looking of the horses.

"Yes, I suppose I should have just pulled my ball point out of my trouser pocked and scribbled it on a take out receipt I found in my wallet." The demon retorted with a scoff.

"Why not, then." Said Past, confused as usual.

"Shut up you half witted horse. When will Charon be getting back?" said Ankou.

"Can't be more than a century or so, old fellow. He has charges wandering the shore that'll want taking over." Said Naberius.

"A century. Really." The charge of Death finally spoke.

"Not that long really. Chin up. I'll have to be along. I have a five o'clock drowning, a five fifteen suicide, and a tanker explosion at half past. It's already five of, so I must be on my way." Ankou said; locking his large wicked-looking scythe into place at the side of the coach his horses drew.

"Wait. Can't this guy take me? I've been a good man. I've done many great things. I'm a philanthropist for Christ sakes!!! I am looking forward to my just reward! I've spent my whole life buying it!" said the Charge

"I suppose, if you want, though he's not sure of the way. If you have been such a great man, just wait a bit, have a sit down, chat with some of the poor wayward souls on this side of the river. Trust me; you don't want to be taken the wrong way. I've seen the 'wrong way'." It seemed Ankou's dry bleach-white bones rattled in a small shudder.

"I don't want to wait here in purgatory with people who aren't sure of themselves, or the poor that couldn't afford proper burial. I am OWED something!" Said the charge.

"Suit yourself... Neberius! Neberius, old chap would you care to take this man to his just reward?"

"I would do my damnedest," Neberius snickered, "Damnedest, get it." If purgatory had crickets they were very audible at that moment. "Ahem, I say, of course I don't know the way at all, so it's a bit of a crapshoot."

"I don't care. I want to get away from this wretched place! All the paupers milling about. Really!" said the charge with a raise of his nostril as he hurried to board the ferry, making a wide birth around any wayward soul that crossed within ten feet of his path.

"Alright then. You've taken your fate into your own hands. You've made your choice. May you find your reward." Ankou said as he swung himself into his driver's seat and grasped the reins that, by the by, looked as if they were made from catgut, or peoplegut... "Get on you brigands; we have to be in Surrey in two minutes." With that he lashed the reins once and was gone before the leathery "crack" died away.

"Right then, left or right sir?" Said the demon known as Neberius.

"Right. For that's what I've done by the poor wretched and unfortunate of the world. Bought them blankets, second had mind," Neberius nodded as the Charge spoke, "Fed them, broth and bread, and given them places to stay, provided they work in my shops making lovely designer clothes. I've been a great man!"

"I'm sure you have as well," said Neberius, "I'm sure you have."

A while passed, and the boat began to slow in front of a set of gates. The gates seemed to be made from human bone and skulls, and the gatekeeper was large and naked with soot colored skin. His horrifically plump yet muscled body was furred from nose to crotch it seemed, and his large flaccid penis was only dwarfed by the spear he held, which seemed to be on fire.

"Your stop, I believe." Said Neberius.

"Those gates don't look very pearly, and he doesn't look much like Saint Peter..." said the Charge.

"I suppose not." Said the crane-demon "Well, please return your trays to their upright position, thank you for riding Afterlife Ferry Service. Enjoy your just rewards."

As the Charge walked up to the gates, the keeper quickly and matter-of-factly impaled him upon the burning spear, said in a voice at once like a scream and a growl, "Welcome to your eternal Just Reward!" and just as nonchalantly tossed him over the gate.

As the form of the stork melted into the form of a man with an oil-stained girdle and long unkempt beard, Charon shrugged to the gatekeeper. "They always think they deserve heaven."

"Except the ones who do." The gate keeper replied as he wiped his spearhead on the brimstone at his feet.

TOGETHER IN BLACK

Ancestors kicking through my head
Trying to convince they are not dead
I suppose they live on in my brain
Giving me knowledge I can't explain
The words that I know are dusty, old
The lives they lived, took, bought, sold
For better or worse they are pieces of me
Helping to mold who I am and will be
I strive to learn from their mistakes
Not to repeat their various heartaches
I breath in smoke, out a clean vapor
Try not to choke, put it down on paper
So live, live on in my newer meatsack
Until the day we're together in black

FIRST OF MANY

The black plastic bag limped and shuffled along the pavement like a wayward old traveler. Wrinkled and caked in dust. I watched it limp past me as I rolled along the sidewalk, dropped off by some girl a half a block on and I was already running out of steam. I hit a crack in the sidewalk, faltered then fell flat of my face and wobbled a bit, then settled. I was quickly picked up by a smart looking man in a business suit and carried off toward downtown. My name is Thomas D. Nineteen-Ninety-Nine. So I'm told. Dressed all in silver, in God we Trust.

The smartly dressed young man passed me on to a street vendor, who gave him a hot dog. He said he had to be off to a meeting or something. I stayed with the street vendor for the rest of that day. He dropped me into a bag that smelled of vinyl and dumped me at the bank, along with some others. Some of them all done up in green and beige and other colours, others done in copper or gold, many done up in silver as I was. I spent the night there, next morning I was put in a tube packed face to tail with two others called

Thomas that looked just like me, it was strange, but, after two days like that, our tube was forcibly busted open against a hard surface, and we were spilled into a compartment in a large drawer. We had a few meaningful conversations about where we had been and what we had done in our lives that day, some older, some younger than me, all with at least a couple good stories. There was an old man, solid and silver, who had been in this race since 1903. He had been in the collection of a boy in 1947, and had watched that boy grow old and silver himself, then slowly fade away. One day they wheeled him on a new bed out the door and he never came home. When found in his case by the man's child, my friend from 1903 said he was spent buying a biscuit in a bake shop. Then it was back to the frantic life he had not experienced in over half a century. I spoke of my ten years on the earth, and how I longed to be in a case on a wall.

Later that day I was given to some young man who carried me off and dropped me nonchalantly in the console of his automobile. I stayed there for three days before I was joined by young Abe. All shiny and dressed in copper, his copper hair and eyes gleamed in the sunlight. We were there for a couple of weeks, having conversations that sometimes stretched into the night. I still think of him now and again, I suppose I was in love with him. As much as someone of my profession can allow themselves to be, seeing as how attachments are always fleeting to us.

At the end of those couple weeks, I was handed into a window to a young be-pimpled man, who dropped me into a compartment in yet another drawer. I was there for literally a minute, I didn't even have time to strike up conversation, until I was passed on to an older gentleman who put me into the pocket of his jacket. I spent the night there amongst lint and used tissues. It was very lonely and the man lived alone.

The very next day was to be the first day of the rest of my life. The man pulled me out of his pocket and handed me to a smiling woman behind the counter who said "Thank you so very much, please fill out that card to tell us how we've done, and bring the coupon back in for your free item!" She then turned to a man who was standing close by holding myself, two fine looking young ones named George, and one small copper clad fellow that reminded me so much of young Abe, (This fellow's name was Abe as well, but he was considerably older.) out on her palm and showed us to the man. She said, in very excited tones. "Our first sale!"

"You know what that means." The man said holding up a wall-mounting case he brought from under the counter.

He neatly matted and framed us all together on a wall by the front door. On our case it said "Pray We Are First of Many!" and that is where I hang today, shining out at all who pass, and we were first of many. Many that are on their journeys now, may they find a home as I have.

THE NEW GOLDEN RULE

I hate demanding, overbearing, demeaning people
You don't have to be hateful to succeed
The idea of stepping on others as you ascend a ladder
Is just a tenet of carelessness and greed
I hate people who don't ever look at the wider world
    around them
Individualism has become a disease
We don't care about others to protect ourselves from
    others
We fear they will do as they please
Because we know that's what we would do when
    the same
Situations present paranoia
Because we assume they'd do us the way we'd
    do them
That's the new golden rule for ya
So try some mindfulness of others on your daily
    routines
Let's try to do some more care

Think of others, it's cliche, and what you'd want them
    to do
And try to strike balance fair
See, they say justice is best when the lady herself is
    blind
But I don't think that's true
I think the most egalitarian way to treat the others
    around you
Is the way you'd want for you

NO SUCH THINGS

"But mummy, I'm afraid. Please leave the shade on!" said Tenotly.

"Now Tenotly, you know you are getting to be a big bruteling. You are getting too old to sleep with a day-shade! There's nothing in the light that's not in the dark!" said Tenotly's mom.

"Except for angels and fairies and people." Tenotly said with a shiver as he pulled the bedclothes up just under his eyes.

"For the last time there are no such things as people!" With a stern glance she slammed the ramshackle door to Tenotly's cave.

The daylight from his roughly hewn window spilled in over him and he shuddered, pulled his cuddly troll toy "Baeem" closer and pulled the cover over his head. Just outside his window, he thought he heard laughter coming from the big house on the hill which was visible from his room, but he just cuddled in deeper and covered his ears.

———

"But mommy, I'm afraid. Please Leave the light on!" Said Timothy.

"Now Timothy, you are getting to be a big boy. You are too old to sleep with a night-light! There's nothing in the dark that's not in the light!" said Timothy's mom.

"Except for demons and goblins and monsters!" Timothy said with a shiver as he pulled his bedclothes up just under his eyes.

"For the last time, there are no such things as monsters!" With a stern glance she slammed the whitewashed door to timothy's room.

The moonlight from his high clean window spilled in over him and he shuddered, pulled his cuddly bear toy "Ben" closer and pulled the cover over his head. Just outside he thought he heard howling coming from the cave at the edge of the woods which was visible from his room, but he just cuddled in deeper and covered his ears.

OUR SONG AS A WORLD

Our song as a world
Is best sung with all voices
Our song as a world
Is best heard with all ears
Our song as a world
Is best felt with all feelings
Our song as a world
Is best shed with all tears

MALAISE AND ENNUI

Despair sat in her rocking chair on the front porch of the cosmos. She knitted storm clouds together into beautiful blankets of deepest, darkest, gloom. She smiled as she watched her sister Chaos dance, glide, and rage through the universe, especially on a little planet called Earth. She watched her cousin Strife and Famine, and her uncle War, not really causing, but gently nudging the world deeper into her own arms. She smiled more broadly. She was so proud of her family. So proud. They all did their jobs flawlessly with the deft hands of experts, except, her own children.

She had twins, a daughter and a son. Malaise and Ennui weren't the children Despair had always hoped for. Malaise sat around all day under an old dead tree in a graveyard in a Portland, Oregon reading Sylvia Plath and Emily Dickinson, thinking about funerals, hospitals, and grocery store queues, the most depressing parts of life. She checked her smart phone periodically and sent a SnapChat or deleted someone from her Facebook for disagreeing with her, or just for being too happy. Malaise was, to the few humans she had met, the most depressing girl they had ever seen.

Ennui spent his days in an internet cafe in Santa Monica, commenting on YouTube and Reddit about the futility of modern life on his MacBook Pro, wearing his American Apparel t-shirt and his Sperry boating shoes while drinking a designer, organic, half caf, soy, Chai Vente latte. Whenever an actual person speaks to him, he quickly runs them off with his regurgitation of Nietzsche and Richard Dawkins. Even though his mother is a goddess and he, himself, a demi-god born of human apathy and Despair herself, he is an atheist, because it is trendy and they are so oppressed. His posts online are filled with "trigger warnings" and NSFW tags, because they are so deep and philosophical that the "mainstream" doesn't get it, man. They just don't. He is not just a petty, selfish, self-important, sex-crazed sociopath. He's a visionary, and being a visionary is painful, bro!

Despair watches her children and their daily lives and she is saddened by their lack of contribution, of effect on the world around them. If only they could cause just a few people to do– Wait. What's this? Despair notices a young girl sitting alone in her room, she is talking to a friend on Skype and listening to some very depressing music in the background (Despair makes a note, she is going to have to start a new Pandora station for this band. Pandora. "Hmm, I wonder how her box is?" Despair digresses. Back to our regularly scheduled gossip session...). The young girl begins to relate a story to her friend.

"Like, my mom doesn't even understand me." Says the first girl.

"Oh Emm Gee, I fuhreeking know. My mom is such a

total curmudgeon about things. I can't even." Says the second girl.

"I know, like, I am just dripping with malaise here but she just doesn't get it. She tells me how privileged I am. Like, how not 'every teenage girl has the money to have an iPhone and a car,' puhhhhleeze. My iPhone is only a fuhreeking five ess and my car is a tahwenty-freeking-thirteen. They're both like, two years old now. I was a babe of fourteen when this car rolled out new. Eww." Says First Girl.

"Ugh, I know. It's so disgusting. My iPhone is a six, but not a six plus. Mom was all, 'Why does such a little girl need such a big phone,' and I was all, 'So it's at least as big as everyone else's, Ma. Jeezus,' She doesn't get it."

"Mine either. I am so in despair right now." Firsty finished as she flopped backward on her bed clutching her chest.

Despair put down her knitting. She walked into her cosmic house and slipped into a little Caucasian number. Blonde with striking features, sunglasses, black dress, and floppy black hat. She called it her Jessica Lange outfit. The resemblance was there. She then popped into a little cemetery in Portland, Oregon. As she appeared in a puff of depressing smelling smoke, Malaise looked up from her reading (It was something about shades of grey, Despair thought she would look into this later, it sounded delightfully depressing.).

"Hello, Mother." Malaise sighed.

"Hello yourself, you little scamp. I sat up there for years knitting rainy days and darning discouragement thinking that you and your brother had done nothing to contribute to the family business, but look at you!" Despair was almost laughing with happiness.

"Yeah. Whole generations of people who don't care about anything but themselves. It's not exactly news, Mom. What's the big deal?" Malaise went back to her reading.

"What's the big— The big deal is this. You have found a whole new way to cause despair! It is a new kind of despair altogether. I think I need to go back to college or something!"

"Congrats, Ma. While you're there, can you drop off these bad professor evaluations to Ennui so he can post them to ratemyprofessor.com? Also, can you go now. I need to get back to brooding. Thanks."

Despair popped across the country to Santa Monica to visit her son and brag about his sister's accomplishments. She was only a little taken aback by her daughter's devil-may-care attitude, mainly because she was so happy not to have raised two good-for-nothings. As these thoughts were flowing through the caverns of her brain like fresh rain water from the mountains of success, she stopped in amazement. There seemed to be a ton of carbon copies of her son around her. Listening to portable record players, leaning against scooters and drinking from metal flasks, or crying in front of art-house movie theatres as they talked of their goings on, saying things like:

"That film was so full of ennui. It made me feel such beautiful despair."

or

"In this album you can really taste the artist's pain. The ennui courses through my veins and leaves me with a grey and foreboding desperation."

or

"So I stopped by the side of the road, cranked my Hi-8 a few times and shivered with ennui as the tears ran down my face. I despaired that the sunset I was filming could be mankind's last if North Korea decided to push one button."

Despair smiled widely. She walked into the coffee shop her son was in, she was now clad in flannel and short khaki shorts, red hair hanging to her waist. A t-shirt under her flannel featured three wolves baying at a moon made of what looked like quinoa. Ennui stood, a tear coming immediately to his eye in a overly practiced fashion. He embraced his mother deeply and wept openly. He stepped back, quickly clicking the iLife camera on his Mac to life. He spoke, "This is my mother. She birthed me, and from her I began. I came to her not in a flood of blood and placenta, but in a cascade of melancholy. I sucked from her bosom the knowledge of dashed hopes and grew into despondency. This is the she. This. Is. She." The room erupted into applause, tears now staining many faces.

"Revel in the beautiful sorrow together, my brother!" Yelled one bespectacled youth, his mustache curled perfectly.

"Do you know all of these people? Have you told them about me?" said Despair.

"Not before just now, Mother, and yes, I know them. We share our spectacular gloom together. We despair together, Despair," He winked.

"I thought all of these years that you just sat here on this computer contributing nothing to your family," Despair looked at her son in smiling disbelief.

"I did sit here, Mom, but as I sat here I created a new kind of despair through internet trolling, cyber bullying, helicopter parenting, social media zombies and dubstep. I have made your job wireless, Mom," He smiled.

"Well, what can I say except, 'carry on with the good

work'? Here, your sister gave me this," Despair handed her son the flash drive Malaise had given her, "She seemed to think you'd know what it is."

"Oh, I do. Thanks mom." He hugged her a long moment, stepped back and announced, "My womb!!!" The room erupted again.

Despair just smiled and waved as she blinked away in a puff of smoke.

"Did I mention she's an illusionist?" Ennui said to the room of shocked spectators who erupted into flannel and American Apparel clad applause for the third time in ten minutes.

As Despair returned to her porch, she sat down to her knitting with refreshed purpose, fired up YouTube, and watched fail videos long after the sun had gone to the other side of that little rock called Earth below. She smiled as she looked on, realizing that her two children were not only worthy, but innovative. She pumped one fist in the air, framed her eye with two fingers, whispered 'Swaaaaag!' quite loudly, and continued to knit, content.

THE BETWEEN TIMES

When I was a child and I knew something was
coming that I wouldn't like, I'd focus on the
between.
That transitory space where you wait and prepare,
knowing something will happen soon.
I would inspect the baseboards as I lay on the floor,
looking for details I'd not yet seen.
I would stare at the ceiling writing stories in my head
about the patterns in the plaster.
I would focus on the minutia of the moment to protect
myself from what was to come.
As I grew older, I learned this is a symptom of
dissociation, and was told it was escapism.
Everyone views these two things as bad, but I don't
understand why.
How is it bad that we use our own minds, controlling
their function to help us slow down and think and
cope and prepare and maintain and...
Breathe.

No matter what the talking heads or therapists say, I
will always be thankful for those quiet, intimate
moments where I allowed my brain to spin into
trivia to help me forget and fortify for some
possible-trauma to come.

I might have to wake up in the morning and deal with
bullies and torment, but for now the pulsing red
alarm clock has lines that blink their beveled
edges to the next minute, and I don't have to know
what time it is to watch them thrum then sharply
rearrange.

I might have to see family members that are just
going to talk about how fat I've gotten, or how
much of a fuckup my mom is in a couple of hours,
but for now the pressure treated plywood under
the edge of my freeflow waterbed looks like a
jungle of tan, sienna and burnt umber ferns and
smells like ozone and newness.

I might have to go to a thankless corporate job
tomorrow, but right now my wife breathes
peacefully as her fan drones and the dogs snore
and the ceiling fan turns its long shadow arms
across the ceiling.

Right now is timeless, forever, holy eternity until I fall
asleep, or mom says we have to go or I realize
what time those elongated, wavering crimson
diamond-lines represent and realize I must force
my eyes to close.

Close on eternity and return to man-whipped reality
where the between doesn't matter, until the next
time it does.

THE CURMUDGEON

"There once was an old curmudgeon,
A miserly old fellow was he,
He hoarded his money his whole life,
Then abruptly fell into the sea."

Wiley Taft was known to his town only as "The Old Curmudgeon of Winderly Way". He lived in a ramshackle old hut at the end of an overgrown street somewhere in a cold New England someplace. Wiley had once had a family, though no one could remember when. He had once been happy, generous, and kind, though no one could imagine how. He was the sourest old man possible. When kids came around to sell candy bars for fundraisers, he booby-trapped his lawn with smoke bombs and bear traps.

Billy Morgan found that out the hard way during a band fundraiser in ninth grade. He dropped a whole box of Almond Delight Bars accidentally from the wagon he was wheeling behind him when he hit a bump in the gnarly old lawn at the end of Winderly. When they hit the ground, a loud snap issued forth as the unforgiving steel teeth of a Bear-Nabber 3000 snapped shut around the chocolate and almond confectionery. Billy Morgan's wagon was not seen until the following week when it showed up on his front lawn, tied in a neat bow, with a note taped to it. Scrawled in barely legible letters it read, "Next time it won't be chocolate and nuts that my trap gets. It'll be flesh and bone."

This was when people stopped going near Wiley Taft's house. One night, though, a traveler came knocking at Wiley's door asking for shelter from one of those famous New England squalls. She was young, beautiful, and charming. She smiled brilliantly at the old man and offered him an embrace. Wiley told her to get bent and to "Do it somewhere that ain't this where," before slamming the door in her face. The enchantress just crossed her arms and nodded. She was gone in a POOF of purple smoke.

The very next day, Wiley was having a breakfast of prunes and oyster juice when, through his open window, a beautiful amethyst feathered seagull flew in. It landed on a stack of money Wiley had been absently counting as he broke his fast. It scooped a shiny new penny up in its beak and swooped back out the way it came. It flew to a buoy about ten meters off shore (Did I fail to mention that Wiley's house, sitting at the end of Winderly Way, was perched precariously atop a cliff above the roaring, icy waters of the northern Atlantic Ocean? Well it was. So that's cleared up.) and alighted, tapping the penny and giving Wiley the best mocking stare a seagull can. Wiley roared, as best a crochety old curmudgeon that eats nothing but prunes and oysters could, and launched himself out of his window. He landed with a thump on top of his waste bins, scattering prune packages and oyster shells everywhere. A few bruises, cuts, and many curses later, he fought his way to his feet, sliding on mother-of-pearl shells and yellow, green, and purple prune wrappers that were glistening slick with morning rain. He squelched in the mud as he trundled headlong toward the bird. He thought, just about the same time his right foot left the edge of the cliff, that he probably should have realized he was stepping off a cliff in the first place, before he did so. As he fell, all he could think of was the fact that some good-for-nothing lazies would likely get his money. They might buy happy fun things and even laug— Those thoughts were cut off by his sudden impact with sharp rocks and, of course, his instantaneous bloody death.

Wiley was found the next morning, following an anonymous tip, mangled on the rocks below, a single shiny penny lying on his forehead. The epitaph on his tombstone read, "2 Chp 4 Vwls" and, after the priest read Wiley's final rights to one lone woman in a lilac dress, the priest asked the young woman if she had anything to say. Ten short words she said before she erupted into a plume of lavender smoke, "He had all the cents, but all the wrong sense." Before the wind blew away the last wisps of periwinkle, the priest heard one last refrain:

"He turned his own daughter away at the door
what a sad old curmudgeon was he?"